IMPERIO

Dante J. Martinez

CHAPTER 1

It was so well made that it could have been a professional's, David thought to himself. His eyes were transfixed on each character, so organized, so detailed and enticing. After all the long hours spent locked inside a prestigious auditorium, this was his only crowned achievement.

"I KNOW this one will work. It has to."

An uncontrollable tap from his right foot began to slap his ears, calling his nervous dark brown eyes underneath the hand me down-makeshift desk. David Chen wrote his resume a fourth time after countless rejections from the previous submissions by state-wide prospects. He wanted resurrect his confidence, despite the reputable institution he attended. Earning a college degree at 19, and earning an associate degree while still in high school, is not something heard about very often.

"A college degree," as David recollected in his father's words, "...is nothing more than a business deal."

From his own transaction, the young buck had wound up with handfuls of debt and not a touch of success. It was most difficult to maintain a healthy mental state.

"That SOB was right," David mumbled under his breath. The words were sour on his tongue. His nostrils flared over a curled lip. He hated his father, especially when his father was right. Growing up, it was like his father could do no wrong, only David; now, it seemed as if things hadn't changed in the slightest.

David recalled the pungent scent of tobacco that followed his begetters every scolding, fueling the distaste for Robert Chen. He desperately wanted to prove to the old stubborn goat that he was deserving of triumph; that he was deserving of becoming a top chef. But the likelihood of triumph faded more with every passing day.

Broke and weighed down by long service hours, David submitted his last effort to a new job listing site: 4jobs.com; hoping to get noticed and escape his current employer, *Waffles & Crepes*.

"It's not too bad," David always reassured himself.

"It could always be worse."

It could always be worse. David thought about his current position. At least the pay was enough to afford most of his rent for a small-studio apartment off Capitol Hill, only a twenty-minute drive away, at most.

"Dammit."

Swollen fingers collapsed the monitor, his tender eyes drew back under the desk, dreading the time to come. David's morning shift was starting in a few minutes, and it couldn't be more of an inconvenience to him. Although David sought a release from this prison of stress, it was the only reason he was still going to work; even if that meant a day filled with cleaning dirty dishes and tables.

Slumped shoulders rolled around the head of his bench. David's eyes wandered throughout the minimalistic bedroom looking for his car keys. The aged-wooden floor creaked under his weight as he raised from the torn-leather chair.

"Where the heck are my keys?!" David questioned out loud. 400 square feet was enough to survive, but not enough to misplace anything important. His vision darted to every corner and frame, countertop and surface, but he couldn't find it anywhere.

Black shadows crept into his peripherals but evaded his direct sight. A cold breath lightly touched the back of his neck and jolted the hairs to a sharp degree. The only fire that had kept the young man warm was his own heightened fear of being extremely late, and his baffled rage over his absent keys. One misplaced step led David's barefoot straight into the hardened column of the table and popped his hallux in an instant. While the young man shrieked, his eyesight dropped once more under the skirt of the desk, noticing his lost goods.

"WHA-a?" A muffled wail of pain and confusion had escaped David's mouth, "...I-ah I don't remember putting you there..."

His throbbing-right toe lightly pressed back down onto the wooden floor. Questions raced through David's mind and caused his brows to tighten, straining the nerves.

"Why didn't I see them earlier?"

The only solid answer David could slab together was him needing a few extra hours of sleep. His sweaty and clammy hands drug across his forehead, attempting to calm the red-pulsating appendage below. He then redirected his heavy gaze one last time under the desk, but this time it was different: very peculiar and extremely unpleasant...

A dimly lit-featureless face was resting by the box stretcher with a long smile and hollowed out eyes. He couldn't unsee it. It was something from a nightmare that wanted David to capture it in the right moment. A visibility like that of a faint puff of smoke or a fleeting mist.

"What WAS that?!?" He thought aloud; the last word cracking from his chapped lips. David's right calf then began to twitch, along with the arch, until his entire leg curled into a agonizing cramp. However, he remained unfazed and rather convinced that what he experienced was a result of sleep deprivation.

A mere hallucination, right? And like that, he fooled himself. The horrible image was gone in the blink of a teary eye. David exhaled unsteadily as if he had awoken from a epileptic seizure and on the fourth deep breath he managed to readjust his posture and straighten out his leg.

"Yeah, I need some coffee."

He dipped down and cautiously reached under the table only to hastily rip his keys out. David flung his body back into a stumble. Goosebumps contagiously spread throughout both his arms and back that left a numbness comparable to a shingle itch. After a long and dark blink, David found himself driving out from his crooked parking, and reversing into the brisk Colorado air. The day was still dreamlike, and the only thing the boy was truly sure of, he was going to be late.

CHAPTER 2

It's the damnedest thing.

The swelling of one's anxieties and thoughts. A realization that we are unable to escape the inevitable. This primal frustration towards the restriction of time and our misapprehension of similar existential factors, plummets the mind into an abyss of despair.

Through the grey haze of the late morning, David had arrived at these notions while pulling into his crammed-employee parking space. Both cars beside him overcrowded their area and breached his due to their crooked angles. Although he recognized the vehicles and who had owned them, it only deepened his vexation. Slightly opening his driver side door, David squeezed out in a frustrated panic and accidentally bumped into the detailed body of the 2012 Chevrolet Camaro parked to his left. Blue paint was scraped toward the dent, leaving a white and grey ripple on the red vehicle. Not even a clean wipe would save David from this problem, which the owner will undeniably notice.

A nervous warmth brushed over David's round face as his eyes met a fellow employee. A much older and skinnier man, Matt, who was taking a smoke break outside the restaurant and staring coldly at David. Without a sign of hesitation or affable familiarity, the crepe chef continued to glare during his two long drags before heading inside. Even though the situation left David cemented in place, he had hoped Matt would be sympathetic enough to remain silent or forget the small incident all together; but deep-down David knew that no one would reserve kindness for him. Some truths are better received when they are not contemplated prior, rather, experienced firsthand to minimize the damage.

Upon entering the eatery, David was harshly greeted by a former friend, Jessica: the main hostess. Her creased brows and squinted green eyes said it all, detailing David's constant inadequacy and her disappointment. Yet, all he could see was the forgotten beauty and his longing for her tender-heartedness.

"YOU'RE LATE Davy."

That name flooded back years of memories together, outside the restaurant when on their off time. Before she came to work with him, before she met…

"You know Aza is looking for a reason, right? This could be the day he kicks you out if you're not smart. So get your shit together!"

Aza. That name was pure gasoline to David's fire. A name that generated hate like his father's. Every uneasy muscle wanted David to throw up his hands and scream that he didn't care, but he reserved some strength, and shrugged Jessica off. Walking to the dimly lit back room, David noticed a shadow creeping into his peripherals, but when he quickly turned his head, Jessica reappeared in his vision.

Standing 5'5" with strawberry blonde hair, Jessica Caulfield was the confrontational type. Always expressing her feelings and thoughts in a brash manner, sometimes without consideration. Jessica never wanted to leave a conversation unfinished, however, a lot was left unsaid between David and her, to the point every encounter needed additional contextualization.

"What's wrong? Did I upset you?" Jessica's tone changed into a perturbing plea.

"No." David sighed. Holding back all his uneasiness. He could see that she still cared, at least some part of her, and maybe she was sorry for what happened. Just maybe.

"Davy, you can talk to me." Her eyes widened in anticipation for one honest answer, but David didn't feel motivated in the slightest.

"Why do you still call me that?!" David sneered. His entire reaction caught her off guard.

"I..."

"It's catchy, don't ya think?" roared Aza while wrapping himself around an uncomfortable Jessica. When Aza Erebros moved, it was the heavy speed that seemed to be the exclusive domain of all large and plump men. His pale bratwurst like fingers always twirling and touching excessively, but his favorite toy was Jessica and her youthful frame.

"And ya look like Davy-Davy Jones, right?! Ha!"

Aza's jokes were intolerable. His desperate call for attention sickened David in the cruelest manner. It was as if Aza knew he was able to puppeteer everyone who worked under his thumb, twisting their lives with his strings and words. If his pungent cologne didn't give that away, maybe it was the ridiculous gold chain he wore outside his collared pollo. Most of all, it was the contemptuous smile Aza always had when he knew he was about to ruin someone's day. A perfect parting of the lips with easy eyes resting low and calm to fully display his yellow teeth. He took pleasure in his outspoken bitterness to the point it swelled his bulge.

"Speaking of, you mind if we chat real quick champ?" His fat hand slapped onto David's shoulder, asserting control. Jessica, now free from Aza's grasp, faded out of the conversation cautiously. Her eyes were full of worrisome regret. Nevertheless, David knew he couldn't escape, so he lowered his head and eyes into submission, assuming the worst.

"What's up Aza?"

David refused to make eye contact. He didn't want to show Aza the satisfaction of intimidation.

"So, bud, I realized last night that you gotta little extra in your pay last month."

This was a huge shock because David didn't notice a raise or any additional income. If anything, he had just enough to get by. His eyes widened as he slowly came to terms with what his boss was suggesting.

"Well you probably did, and well that's because I didn't take out taxes. So, for this next pay I gotta take double. You get that, right? Just following the rules man."

A nerve was pinched behind David's eye, causing an uncontrollable twitch.

"You piece of shit." David thought quietly to himself. His fists curled and cracked, sending an aftershock throughout his arms and shoulders.

"Also…"

To David's disbelief, he wasn't done. What more could he want?

"Matt told me you came in late and scratched Red Baron getting out of your car."

"That son of a BITCH!" David yelled internally. He knew that decrepit chef was a dirty snitch, and what made it worse, Aza was referring to his Camaro as Red Baron as if it needed a name.

"Now, I ain't mad, but I will be taking out what you owe right away, so there's no confusion in the future. Cool?"

Pure rage overflowed David as his sore eyes struck upon Aza's tranquil expression.

"Cool." David exhaled.

"Awesome Davy, I knew you'd understand! And uh, first thing before you start on the tables, could you take out the trash and call Vincent? He's later than you today which ain't like him."

White arms rolled to Aza's side trouble free.

"Sure Aza." David's eyes reverted away.

"Thanks bud! Now go, go." Aza shooed David away as he turned back around to Jessica who was watching from behind the counter.

David slowly trekked into the kitchen and avoided Matt altogether to lift the foul black bag. His legs numb and weightless. He could feel the narc leer but sought complete avoidance. Still, there it was again, the creeping darkness. The shadowy figure caught in his optical fringe. Why was it following him? That terrifying face. A ghostlike man that watched from the corner of the scullery. David could still be tired and stressed to the point he was hallucinating this apparition, but from his house all the way to his work? Further, the more David thought about it, the more its entire existence vanished from his sight and mind.

"What's going on with me?" David questioned himself. Mondays usually carried dread and misfortune, but today it was unforgiving. He felt as if he was going crazy, and all it took was Aza to cast him off the ledge.

A dirt covered converse found the broken pavement as he exited from the kitchen back door to the alley. Catapulting the shifting bag over and onto his trap, David slowly shuffled to the open green dumpster. The entire alley smelled like fermented urine and had multiple gang taggings on the aged brick wall. Denver's cultural touchstone. Then all of his tense thoughts came to an immediate end. David became distracted by a high-pitched buzzing sound, breaching the roof of the building. Above it, hovered a remote-controlled pilotless aircraft, moving around the complex.

"Who knew people on Broadway would start playing with drones…" David pondered. His knowledge towards rapid technological innovation provided enough reasoning, and due to economies of scale, anyone could buy a drone for as little as $60. Nevertheless, it was odd because traditional drones have been limited to military use due to high costs, and this device had incredible technical sophistication.

David then remembered Aza's additional request. He groaned, "I have to call him."

After throwing the putrid sack into the wide bin, David's inflamed fingers whipped out his cellphone and flicked over to his contacts. Vincent, poor Vincent. The small dark-man was a state-native but seemed foreign with his accent and body language. First meeting, David could've sworn Vincent was from Morocco, mainly from his gestures of affection; but Vincent Rivera was just a Boulder hippy, a self-proclaiming expert of free love. Most of his fond liberation was influenced by his overconsumption of marijuana. Nonetheless, there was a dark side to Vincent. Some days when he clocked in to serve, you could visibly see the depression behind his eyes. Perhaps Vincent's spirituality was his outcry for endearment. Whatever the reason, Vincent's absence will not go over well with Aza, who will probably blame David for not reaching him properly.

Still, David could see Vincent's alleged reason to abandon this job. *Waffles & Crepes* was a dead end, especially with people like Aza running the place. Since David started working there has been a noticeable decline in customers. So much that Aza considered a rebrand and changed the menus to generate new business. It was almost sad really. A lot of lives were tied up to this establishment, and even on an average day like today, there hasn't been a single client.

What hope and support did David truly have other than himself? Was that truly enough? These lonesome revelations could either make or break a man, and David was truly bent at the seams. If David could only reach his aspiration, then maybe all the suffering would have been worth it and hardened him for the better.

"Or maybe I should smoke weed and become a non-conformist like Vincent." David curtly considered the idea.

Despite each attempt, David couldn't reach Vincent as the dial up jumped straight to voicemail. For all David knew this could be his resignation. Still, David had an unsettled feeling deep inside his gut, not Aza's scornfulness, but a need to check in. Regardless of their vast differences, David had always felt that him and Vincent were connected, whether that be their adverse spirits or their common affliction. He needed to know that Vincent was okay.

On that lingering wish, David managed to reach the set of bells on the caller's phone. An empty chime that echoed beyond his eardrum into the vast abyss. Sending a signal into the void that anticipated an answer back. A deafening silence overwhelmed the alley, which reverberated the mobile toll as it continued blaring after each pause. David's surroundings were so quiet, even the drone had disappeared without a trace. It was as if life had stood still for one moment. Everything suspended in place, including the breeze, up until a faint whisper could be heard. A customary jingle. David's curiosity peaked just as he lowered his device to increase the outside volume.

"Is that…" he had a sudden realization. The sound was coming from around the corner, and along with it, a potent smell. A rotten aroma like spoiled meat with a hint of benzene. Each whiff caused David to gag but he trekked on. His inquisitiveness was more profound than his sensitivity to profane sights and odors. The rattling continued and resonated beyond the rim of the wall, beckoning David to retrieve it. When his fair face peeked behind the glum ridge, David witnessed an anomaly. Even Aza wouldn't be able to comprehend, let alone believe it.

A burning joint laid still beside a cracked, but ringing smartphone covered in a slimy black tar that displayed the caller ID as "David". Next to the phone rested a bent beyond repair-Speedvagen 650B rugged road. Vincent's beloved bike. Its rims were contorted and curled alongside the fragmented spokes which impaled the tires and twined within the dislodged chain.

"What the hell?" He gasped, "Did he get hit by a truck?!"

After David cross-examined what he was perceiving, the call ended. Vincent's laid-back voicemail message welcomed David once again, followed by muteness. A strange oily mucus that covered Vincent's phone was displaced on the cycle's warped frame like finger painting. There was a trail of blood smeared beside the wreckage that led to the brick wall and disappeared. He was completely dumbfounded, but quickly assumed that Vincent had a horrible accident and ran off to get help. If that were the case, then he should be inside the restaurant. Perhaps Vincent was seeking aid from his fellow employees, and god forbid, employer. They could be waiting for David to return.

"This has to be a prank," David affirmed. Trembling thumbs coiled around the blue lit text pad. Ready to redial for assurance until his own device began to jingle. Though David had never seen this caller before, which was a series of 4's displayed as a 10-digit number, he surmised that it was pertaining to Vincent.

"Hello?!" David hastily answered.

A delicate and maternal voice returned: "Hello, David."

Before David was able to question who was calling, the soft feminine voice continued:

"I am calling from *Backyard Diner* located in Idledale off State Highway 74, and after receiving your resume earlier today, we would like to interview you as soon as possible!"

The old church which became a lively restaurant with a rooftop lounge and global small plates was a haven to David. A perfect escape from *Waffles & Crepes*. This was a dream-like scenario resurrecting before his very eyes.

"A-ah, yes! Yes! I-I can meet you. Uh, How soon?" David fumbled out.

"This afternoon between 1 and 4 p.m. would be perfect."

"Perfect!" David repeated with elation.

A click ending with a small but confident smile, David looked beyond the wreckage, to the Rocky Mountain Range. The oddity he noticed beforehand no longer mattered. This was a new beginning, and all he had to do was create an excuse to leave. With a sense of optimism in the air, David was moved to the main entrance with wondrous daydreams. Hoping that when he arrived, he'd be greeted by Vincent. Perhaps David would give him a ride, take him away from this place. Possibly Jessica too. She was sorry, he felt it. Jessica's concern meant enough for David. So he thought…

Such a distasteful show of professional integrity: Aza's meaty hand wiggled between Jessica's thighs. Those sloppy lips pressed against her red and golden locks, but Jessica's eyes rolled in the least bothersome way. It was at this moment David lost all care, and only his self-preservation remained.

"Go-go fuck yourselves!" David yelled as he stormed off. He then ripped his car door open and bashed it into the passenger side of Aza's cherished automobile.

"I don't care anymore." He repeated to himself as he sped away into the early afternoon.

CHAPTER 3

Moving on was easier said than done.

Watered eyes obsessively checked the rearview mirror, searching for remnants that were chasing and pleading for him to stay. Hoping that someone cared, anyone for that matter. But there was no one. Rooted in his chest was a bottomless pit of sorrow, a hole that originated from his childhood now deepened by Jessica.

"I'm such a simp." David muttered to himself as he rounded tight canyonlands during his scenic drive.

"She just used me, and I was dumb enough to let it happen."

David tightened his grip on the steering wheel as heartache overwhelmed his body. It was a poison surging through his veins, but a familiar feeling.

Demons are born from our darker thoughts. Embodying our fears, anger, and pain that resonate from the past; and sometimes, we cling to them because that's all we've become accustomed to. For David's sake, he clung to every hope presented before him in order to flee from his increasing shadow. A black cloud above his crown that epitomized his internal adversary. David was always desperate to find solace in another's brightness, but that backfired at every instance. Yet, this new job position could be his eternal light, a sign to release and let go of his own darkness. Once and for all.

David could feel it as he weaved up beside the gushing stream. A sense of destiny accompanied by a flush of warmth, which was far greater than any moment in his life. Even when he left his father in Hong Kong. This famous Colorado excursion enhanced his sentiment. From what David knew of Idledale, it was quiet, and there was not much in town byways of commerce besides the recently famous restaurant. The establishment was dream-like as it overlooked the drive between Evergreen and the Front Range, capturing the beauty that originally enticed David to live in the colorful state.

However, the unincorporated village had a strange history. Originally known as Starbuck Heights in 1933, the town was hit by a devastating flood, destroying everything, including 20 residents. When it was rebuilt, the name was changed to Idledale, while a church and cemetery were constructed to honor the deceased inhabitants. Curious to think that the only attraction in this sector was for families and locals to pay their respects. A revered house for the dead, until it was bought out and renovated into a popular restaurant.

"Strange," David thought to himself. Nonetheless, the wedge of mountain life within the metropolitan area of Denver was enough to excuse the muddied past.

Any person would be honored to view life up at 6,466 feet in the rolling foothills. A true slice of heaven, and the further David was from *Waffles & Crepes*, the more his head rose in smug confidence. Those he left behind were about to be severed completely from his thoughts and anxieties. All that mattered was the coming interview and the beauty of nature before him. But that could all change.

"What if?" David shakily thought.

Who knows what truly lies ahead. David never did, but how could he? Someone who's tortured past relapsed throughout his timeline? He was right to doubt if destiny ever existed.

A phantom pain outstretched his right foot from the gas pedal and caused a burning sensation around his heel. The bright glow of the afternoon sun distracted this annoyance, and David eased into the last-long turn towards his destination. To David's right, dominated by scattered trees and gnarled shrubs, stood a fine but ruinous white kirk. It was covered by overcast when he arrived and creaked ominously in the howling wind, whipping around the vacant lot. A ray of light reflected from the stained-glass windows into David's eyes, blinding him to exit the vehicle in a hurry.

Empty churches around the world are finding new life as restaurants. These abandoned religious buildings originally were designed to evoke awe and spiritual devotion, but designers have discovered that common elements created impressive dining rooms. Despite specific unifying features, this set up looked entirely different from what David had researched. Not one quality seemed inviting, unlike the other installations which offered a friendly atmosphere. The wood-paneled exterior was in a sad state of disrepair and thick cobwebs hung on every rotted surface. For a popular restaurant occupying a former 20th century church, he had expected some resurrection.

David began to doubt the job's existence all together, until a group of delightful women exited the entrance doors to greet him with open arms and large smiles. The girls were not much older than David, and all were dressed in a white-uniformed polo, apron, and leggings. Every single jane had a name tag and introduced themselves with intense excitement, throwing David off guard. The young ladies grew prettier with each introduction, up to the last, who was in David's honest opinion:

"The most beautiful girl in the world."

The maiden divulged herself as Monica Grey, manager and owner, and welcomed the oriental chap into their home of business. David was entranced and promptly followed them into the historic house of god. He admired the girl's fruitful frames and the vaulted ceilings that were paired with dim lighting. The dining room, awash in jewel tones, oozed old-fashioned formality with white tablecloths, plush dining chairs, and, of course, stained glass windows.

"Do you like it?" Monica whispered into David's ear.

"I set out to retain the original character of the building during restoration, unfortunately we haven't been able to repurpose the exterior at the moment."

Her bright blue eyes studied David's messy, yet straight black hair, and wide cheekbones. His dark orbs scanned the room, absorbing the antiquity of the structure.

"I left the original vaulted ceilings intact for those patrons who want to dine inside and have a divine experience." She added.

"It's quite amazing don't you think?"

Mesmerized by the open kitchen in place of the altar, David inattentively responded, "It's extremely unique. I've actually never been in a building like this one."

"Do you know about this property's history?" Monica raised her eyes with David's.

In a monotone voice David replied, "From what I've read, the church was built after the 1933 flood that destroyed the town."

Monica nodded.

"That's correct. This place was a holy memorial for the deceased. For the 14 taken and never recovered."

"14?" David's ears perked.

"I thought the Denver Post recorded 20?" he proposed in awe.

"Aha yes," Monica chortled, "the 6 were included in the report, but didn't go missing until after the incident. Such strange times. There's a myth that suggests some local war vet had cursed the residents and caused the flood."

David couldn't help but courtesy laugh with the bombshell hostess, who played with her hair and continued:

"The tale goes that a corporal went missing in trenches during the First World War. For years not a single soul had seen him, but everyone was happy that he was gone. The town and military felt the man was a plague, but when he returned, his condition was far worse than before. The vet kept his distance from everyone, and only came out at night. Neighbors worried for years and claimed that he had practiced black magic and spoke to shadows, but those were just scary legends driving fascination and wonder to this small town."

David raised his tiny chin, "How interesting. I never read about that."

A warm and comforting smile spellbound David. Monica's delicate hand softly touched his shoulder.

"You have a unique mind David. We need someone like you here. We need you working in this kitchen."

"I'm happy you called!" David blurted out. His brain scrambled from the invigorating interaction.

"It-it honestly was perfect timing."

"I'm glad to hear that! Do you mind if we go into the confession booths for our interview?" Monica's hand lifted and directed him towards the stalls.

Although incredibly odd to David, he reluctantly agreed, "No, not at all."

"My apologies, this slice of Catholic history goes all the way back to the Middle Ages," Monica explained.

"History is important for a place like this. I get it."

Entering the booth, David sat on a piece of furniture and looked to his left where the grille and curtain resided, which separated the priest from the penitent. The pasty box generated an uneasy feeling, but for all its physical barriers, the cabinet allowed Monica to breath up close to his ear. He was instantly addicted to the atmosphere of crepuscular intimacy. Whether he yearned for it or was hopelessly fond of Monica, David was at her whim.

"So, David, for this interview process I'm going to be asking you a few questions, and then afterwards you'll have the opportunity to ask me a few questions. Is that okay?"

Hesitant, David suddenly realized he never made it to the interview process, even for *Waffles & Crepes*.

"That's perfect, yeah." He slowly answered.

"Alright! To start, if you could change anything about your current situation and job, what would it be?"

"Uh, I uh would…" David tried his best to restrain himself, "I would rather be in an environment where I can grow. It's not that I hate my job or anything like that…"

That was a blatant lie. David felt the weight settle in. He began to fear the simple sin, but it was too late for denial.

"My current job, well they never gave me a chance to prove myself, and that's…"

"That's all you want. I see that passion David."

Monica's intrusion was more than surprising, but David couldn't disagree.

"Yeah, it's all I want."

"Okay well moving on…"

Monica paused. The silence crept in and made David anxious.

"What's your relationship with your parents?"

David would've preferred the silence after hearing those words. Instantly, he witnessed the damaging memories flood his mind, accompanied with a deafening siren.

"David?" A slightly concerned Monica pressed on.

"Fine. I- my parents they…" he couldn't find the right words to express the pain he felt inside.

"My mother died when I was little, she had stage 4 lung cancer."

David mustered all of his strength and carried on.

"My father and I lived in Hong Kong together. I grew up there. He and I, we never got along really. My mother's death was very hard on him, and I just had to leave to become my own person. My mother was from America, so I decided this was my new home."

"He was tough on you, wasn't he?"

For some reason this deeply enraged David. He gritted his teeth and refused to lash out.

"Who was she? A fucking therapist?" David angrily thought, but recalled that this job was his last hope, so he pushed ahead.

"My father wanted life to be a certain way, and it was difficult for him to accept what had happened. I shouldn't hold that against him. I think we all can do that. Some more than others."

"That's very mature of you David."

"Well I'm 19 so it's about time I show that I have grown up."

"19?" Monica said stunned, "I assumed you were 14."

He chuckled, "I get that a lot. Everyone I've pretty much worked with assumed I was younger than them. Still do ha."

"That's a good thing. You'll age nicely."

David blushed at the compliment, but quickly grew sad thinking of Jessica's past admiration. Perhaps Monica could give David the inwardness he so desperately pursued. The affection Jessica would have exchanged for another man like Aza.

"Thank you, David."

"You're welcome." He replied, but suddenly backtracked due to his confusion by the swift sincerity.

"Wait was-was that it, Monica?" David questioned inanely. No reply. The cold stillness rattled under his skin. David couldn't handle it, not even for a minute.

"Monica?" He continued, his worries instantly rolling from his tongue, "Am-am I done?"

As David stood up, the sweet voice returned, "Not yet."

From the open space, in the middle of the aged seating and roughed step, a hand unexpectedly snatched David's right leg, and another dug a jagged blade into his heel bone. The harsh thrust ripped the tendon and calf tissue drenching his foot and stoop. A leathered palm tugged the cold steel up and out of the wailing boy, throwing him down in a frenzy. The mangled lad stumbled in agony and smacked his forehead violently on the ligneous opening. Warm blood sprayed onto the white interior and exterior of the holy cabinet. David seized for a moment as tears and bloody snot drained from his swollen face. His outstretched mouth foamed with yellow bile. Then he was out cold and still as a board between miserable hiccups.

Two large-black mitts aggressively heaved David's body away and left a large puddle of blood. In an out of consciousness, David caught glimpses of armored men carrying him to a lead-lined container covered in rust and decay, labeled No. 4-1. Then David blacked out again. Drifting off to another reality.

CHAPTER 4

When pressured under extreme stress, an individual can experience fitful dreams, far grimmer, and for many, unusually memorable. Changing one's routine dramatically often meant recollecting these deranged hallucinations. For a person who was horribly mistreated, these ghastly apparitions merged with daily existence.

Some visions dramatized the feeling that we are being held hostage by a mysterious predator. Even so, David was truly captive within both realms and the mirage he witnessed ahead was the Western Front, fought by Allies in the trenches. The foxholes were long, narrow ditches that dug into the ground where the infantry rested. Covered in mud with their toilets overflowing, the armed men beamed at David, the foreigner. A great number of the soldiers' feet were exposed, blotched and blistered, which resulted from fighting in the wet conditions. Trench foot was rampant. Too many servicemen to count. Their starved faces resembled death itself. These soldiers would occupy their troughs, offering some degree of protection against machine-gun fire.

Excluding poison gas, but fortunately David knew that many of the gases used in World War I were still relatively weak.

David was on a head trip, but why the Great War? Was this a past life he was witnessing, or a vivid recreation of the dreadful events? Preceding his investigation, a Fokker F.1 triplane rattled in the sky. Its design was lodged somewhere in David's collective memories. A perfect red contrasted with the grey clouds. Four subtle shots rang from below and pierced the fighter aircraft. All at once, troops mounted their attack from the moat, bayonets fixed to their rifles, climbing over the top edge into "no man's land."

Not surprisingly, this approach wasn't effective and led to mass casualties as bodies gruesomely dropped back into the gorge. All David could do was watch helplessly as men defecated themselves in panic, but proceeded to fill the gaps their deceased comrades had left behind. To his horror, the remains returned with open holes and brain matter. Each one far worse than the previous, and the wounds increased in size and disrepair. Still, David couldn't move, and only observed the hellish scene. When the bloodshed halted, David was free to migrate through the pile of corpses. Knee deep in decaying flesh, he was surrounded by audible cries from sappers buried alive beneath the surface. Among the moldering dead, an officer clutched David by the peg and uttered something bizarre:

"D-don-n't t-trus-st C-corporal Lawrence."

Stupefied, David retraced his steps and met a group of stained hands, pulling him under the mound. The officer climbed on top of the frightened youngster and howled, "DON'T TRUST HIM!!"

David fastened his eyes shut and prayed to God for salvation as he sank beneath the perished. Up until he awoke in frigid darkness.

It was a strange feeling. Basking in the nothingness. David strained his optical nerves to see anything before him. Anything at all, but it was a place completely absent of sunlight. The unfamiliarity made David extremely afraid of everything. Although he felt as if he had spent a lifetime there. One resemblance from the normal world was his drumming leg pain, which soaked the floor beneath him. A huge loss of blood drained him of all energy. Simply reaching for the open gash below his calf muscle was too much to handle. Every inclination he possessed was a concern for his own survival.

"SOMEBODY HELP ME!!!" David screamed from the top of his lungs.

No response besides the gut wrenching reverberation.

"SOMMEBODYY!!! PLEAAASEE!!!" David continued as his voice broke into an uncontrollable sob.

His echo was welcomed with overhead breathing. Low and heavy, similar to a deep growl from the belly of a lion. The noise came from behind David, who turned around to be greeted by small spectacles of light. He couldn't make out the objects that flickered in the corner, illuminating the rotten walls covered by dark silhouettes. A huddle of long figures moved up and down in slow synchrony, dancing in the blackness. Before David could repeat his lament, a moist-popping sound answered. Frequent liquid bursts accompanied with shuffling and a nasty gurgle.

Under growing broadcast static, David experienced a new nightmare before him as the luminescence revealed standing bodies that were extremely decomposed and covered in tar, feasting on a fresh corpse. The small glow was situated in their vacant sockets. Caverns that reminded David of the phantom he witnessed earlier. His sight uncontrollably adjusted to the frightful scene and recognized the unfortunate soul almost immediately. Corroded hands tore into the open cavity of the carcass and shifted it closer to David like an offering.

David choked, "V-V-Vincent?!"

An elegant voice transmitted aloft, "106."

"HELLO?!? WHAT WAS THAT?!?" David cried out.

The streaming radio replied, "Their name."

Pierced with terror, David returned his gaze and met the gleam of one of the entities. It's grimy and wrinkly face contorted with a deranged smile. David was unable to utter a single word, almost losing the ability altogether. It's jagged teeth drizzled with blood and forced him to speak.

"PLEASE LET ME GO! PLEASE!" David rejoined horror-stricken.

"No. We need you David. There are a lot of lives depending on us and you."

"MONICA?!? WHAT THE FUCK!?! WHAT THE FUCK DO YOU WANT FROM ME???" David wildly bawled.

Weakness engulfed the adolescent, immobilizing him under the growing crowd. More of them appeared from the sludge displaced on the visible ceiling and wall. Each one similar in appearance and expression; all transfixed on David with a wide-lipless smirk.

"They're attracted to your suffering. It seems only boys and men between the ages of 10 to 25. Depression draws them in like moths to a flame. You see, David, these beings were originally residents, but returned as abominable creatures craving human flesh. Though they're not exceptionally agile, they're able to vanish inside solid matter, entering what we assume to be a pocket dimension..."

"YOU FUCKING MURDERS!!! YOU KILLED VINCENT!!!" David interrupted.

"No." The disembodied voice insisted.

He squalled, "LIARS!!"

"No." After a momentary pause, the transmission resumed: "They retrieved him themselves. That is why you are here. To prevent further attacks."

"WH-Why me?" David whimpered.

"You were their next target. It was only a matter of time. Now that all of them are present, we can begin our next phase. We're sorry David, but this is the only way."

"BURN IN HELL!" He shrieked.

"We thank you for your service. Godspeed."

The alluring relay ended in an abrupt click.

Suddenly David was irradiated by the humanoid's shine. All vision honed on the baited youth. The naked and maggot infested cadavers gradually progressed towards David, who was naturally a deer caught in the headlights. Petrified beyond belief.

"I can't- I can't die like this..."

Shriveled arms reached out for David, beckoning him over, all while grinning from ear to ear. Their steady advancements were a tidal wave of despair, and David refused to believe any of it was real.

"Please, GOD, I CANNOT DIE LIKE THIS!!!"

The closer they were, the louder their crackled groans grew. An utterance of David's name, as if the ghouls knew he would be delivered to them. Their raspy declaration prompted David to soil himself. Death was imminent and all he could do was wait.

"Psssst. Hey, David." A hushed tone called out to the helpless adolescent.

"Over here." It continued.

David looked over his shoulder and saw a little man, pale and in grey tones, dressed with an old army tunic. He was a young and handsome soldier, decorated in the same heavy wool garment as the others from David's brief fantasy, embellished with two chevron insignias. His eyes akin to the encroaching doom that shimmered before David. Adorned with a welcoming twinkle, the serviceman waved David over as he sat crouched by a gaping hole in the ground.

"Over here." He repeated. His long and dirty nail pointed below, urging David to follow him. The monochrome gent descended head first and magically escaped under the floor. Blaring sirens exploded with a flashing red light. An emergency alert for the facility, highlighting the thirteen evil spirits as they drew near. Their hue was a deep scarlet, but their sockets remained jet black and absent of mercy. A willingness to live stirred David, each arm steadily pulling his heavy body to the well. Peering into the inky vortex, David saw a light at the end of a spiral tunnel and the youthful army man on the other side, upside down and calling him over.

David realized his only option, and promptly dove into the spinning gyre. The substance was comparable to wet clay, but more of an adhesive sludge, and relatable to ink. David was covered in the strange mire. Entering every crevice of his body, including eyes and mouth. It dowsed him completely, but he trudged onwards. David was fighting for his life as the wicked creatures soon followed and entered the countercurrent.

Breaching the exit, David could smell a stale fragrance and noticed some neighborly graffiti ahead. It was the alley behind *Waffles & Crepes*. Next to the large dumpster he visited earlier that day. He took one long inhale, and squeezed his core through the swirling threshold as the funnel grew tighter around him. David was inches away from breaking free. One considerable difference was that David departed horizontally, and not vertically like the gateway had implied. Nonetheless, he toppled a foot into the backstreet, his face planting so hard that his lacerated foot bent into the slurry, which tore it further.

Grasping the rough pavement, David suddenly felt an ungodly terror clutch his hacked limb which melted the skin to a sizzle. It was one hand, then two, three- the dread multiplied. Scalding meat hooks had branded David's entire shank, burning it to the bone.

"SOMEONE!!!!! AAAHHHH!!!! HELP ME!!! PPPLEEAAAS-SEE!!!" David bellowed, but no one listened.

Continuous tugging had ripped David up and back into the adjacent depression. His chest reinstalled as the young man braved the edges of the arch, holding himself from instant death.

"Davy."

He looked up in trembling fear. Across on the once scribbled structure, hung an old-irregular man covered in boiling oil. His face split in half with one side an adolescent and the other senile, but joined by one broad smile. In his eroded hand swung Jessica's severed head.

"Goodbye." The old man chuckled as he disappeared into the black mucus that dangled his body.

"NOOOO!!!!" David let out one last scream, before being grisly twisted into the shrunken hole. Blood squirting onto the empty alleyway as the unnatural doorway vanished, along with David.

The maimed kid was plucked back into his cage and feasted on by the thirteen, still alive and suffering. Their mouths feverishly devoured his entrails as he sobbed and begged his father for forgiveness. In David's final moments, he witnessed a white bolt scattering across the sky. It was spreading like his bodily fluids, but magnifying in power. 80,000 lumens of light flooded the area. The blinding energy disintegrated the monsters and poor boy, reducing them to mere atoms in a flicker. David wasn't embraced by angels or the grateful departed, but by oblivion. Unfortunately, many like him will be following suit.

Out of the screeching static a voice answered:

"The D-class individual was unsuccessful at containing all of the Keter-class objects, and the facility is now under lockdown as security and research personnel are transferred to Site Security immediately. Any objects or personnel lost to 106 are to be deemed missing/KIA. No recovery attempts are to be made under any circumstances."

End of the monologue.

CHAPTER 5

Damable actions are committed by everyone. Even the most innocent soul. Yet, to deny knowledge of responsibility is the foulest ability we possess.

This is most common in an organized hierarchy due to a lack of evidence that can confirm if they were personally involved or at least willfully ignorant of the actions. Director Monica Grey was neither as she watched David's death horrifically unfold before her luminescent eyes. She possessed a cold but bright stare, unwilling to act while her female staff beckoned for a response.

"PRESS THE BUTTON!!" They hysterically repeated.

To no avail. The sounds of David's weeps and the gnawing of his bodily organs overwhelmed the control room. Once the boy begged for his father's forgiveness that triggered an emotional response within Monica. She recollected a distant memory of her life in Idledale at the age of 19 with her husband. When she pleaded to her father. Before the foundation, she lived happily with her spouse, who resembled the dying adolescent. It wasn't long until everything she cherished was destroyed. Her entire livelihood became engulfed by fast-moving water. Monica's partner was caught in a low crossing on their escape, which became a death trap to the remaining residents. A whirlpool of black and brown mud buried Monica's loved ones as a harrowing figure levitated above the maelstrom.

A rough hand slammed on the push switch, setting off the wave of light that obliterated the helpless victim and entities below. It belonged to Commanding Officer Blake, a senior member of the foundation, who was more than familiar with the facilities contents.

"We need to evacuate, now."

This stern message caused the security personnel to round up the site staff: researchers, specialists, and the director alike into one unit.

"Site 11 has been compromised, we must relocate to Site 1 immediatley. Officer Trung, make sure the broadcast was relayed to the other sectors on the PA system, including the residential housing and commercial businesses. Officer Mann, make sure everyone who was in the facility is accounted for."

"What about 986?" Mann briefly asked.

"It's currently stored in the Anomalous Document Repository. It's secure." Monica answered.

Blake scoffed, "Faulkner is not my concern. Getting everyone out alive is. Mobile Task Force Operatives will handle it after they deal with 106. That is their main priority. Officer Hawley, take the secured unit to Extraction Zone 5. Officers Winkler and Riggs, protect them at all costs. Director Grey, you're with me."

Officers Mann and Trung separated in the T-shaped hallway, disappearing into their respective rooms. The hardened vet watched the rescue group descend the entrance hall with a thousand yard stare. Monica gazed up at his black uniform adorned with red stripes, biding her time.

He grunted, "Magenta… MTF teams may require extensive planning because of this."

"Are we in deep waters?" Monica queried.

An instant-enraged look flooded the officer's face, "What the fuck do you think?!"

"Officer Blake…"

"Don't act innocent. You forget, I was around for 3001, and I witnessed what others only rumour about. I know you, Director Grey. You're not to be trusted. That boy you sacrificed would've had a better chance without your help. D-Class is for murderers!" Blake protested.

He continued, "For all I know, this was your doing."

Monica was frozen, her eyes submerged to a glacier blue. A single tear dropped down her flushed cheek.

"What do you want from me?!" Monica demanded.

Blake leaned in.

"I just want you to know, if this goes sideways, I'm shooting you first."

The silver haired man whipped his pistol out from the holster and squeezed Monica's shoulder with his leathery glove. The crisp barrel of the SIG Sauer P226 pressed delicately against her back.

"Move." Blake ordered.

"Officer please…"

The gun dug into her spine, rubbing up against her pearl white lab coat. Monica let out a small squeal of discomfort.

"I said MOVE." Blake reaffirmed.

Monica staggered down the hall, catching up to the others as they passed through the security gateway and headed into Checkpoint 1 to start the decontamination process. Blake stayed close behind and waited with Monica while the airlock doors closed in front of them. The officer then extended his palm to Monica while holding her at gunpoint.

"Give me your keycard."

Director Grey nervously shook her head, but a firm nudge of the handgun reasserted Blake's dominance. Tucking her tail, Monica handed over her plastic identification and the rugged face cracked out a snicker.

"You're not leaving my side Director Grey."

Huddled like cattle, the staff and officers anticipated the decontamination gas, but nothing came. It was at this moment, Officer Winkler knew something was wrong. A tingling sensation rose from his gut, feelings far worse than dread.

"Officer Blake. What should we do?" The question vibrated through the thick glass doors, but his superior couldn't answer.

"Office BLAKE. W-What's going on? Why aren't the fumes coming out??" Officer Riggs hollered. His eyes were transfixed on a slimy material gradually coming out from the pipes above.

"OFFICER BLAKE! LET US OUT OF HERE!" Winkler shouted over the growing panic.

Warm blood began to spew from the ducts, spraying onto the screaming crowd. An item shot out of the upper right tube smacking Riggs's helmet. The object was hard enough to cause slight pain, but the befuddled agent quickly picked it up for examination. One glance caused his hands to shake and drop the bloody name badge.

"It-it's Officer Mann's…" he shuddered. More red liquid doused the broken unit. Bits of bone and small chunks of intestines popped out of the hose.

Monica became extremely concerned as she understood the situation at hand. She attempted to turn on Blake, until she noticed his finger on the trigger. At that same time, Officer Hawley tried to keep a few of the researchers calm but was met with flailing arms and punches. It was so overwhelming that it caused the officer to drop her assault rifle.

"Blake please. Use the card, you have clearance." Monica implored.

The gun adjusted to her nape. Blake snarled, "Shut the fuck up! What are up to?!"

"You can't be serious…" She exhaled.

One loud scream caught everyone's attention, and directed it to the open jaw of Hawley. Legs shook and urine leaked from her pants while she stared in terror at the hovering monster. A vest wearing-old man devilishly smiled at the petrified girl before yanking her up into the ceiling and gobbled from the neck down. The pure anguish Hawley faced led Officer Winkler to panic and shoot himself. In an instant, chaos broke out among the group. Officer Riggs aimed his weapon but the two bodies disappeared. Almost in the blink of an eye.

Monica prayed to Blake, "I beg you. Let them OUT PLEASE!! Do what you need to, but PLEASE SAVE THEM DAMMIT!!!"

He held a disdainful glare while surveying Monica's emotional guise. The noise ahead did not matter.

"You lying bitch!"

Blake pointed the barrel between Monica's enchanting eyes, but before he could pull the level, a harsh click startled him. To his right floated Jessica's detached head, which was covered in a black slime that also took the shape of her basic internal organs. She possessed black orbs in her cavities, but worst of all, she had numerous fangs that punctured through her cheeks and lips.

Before the doyen could act, the beast gorged on his face, causing Blake to misfire and hit the sealed door. The bullet grazed Monica's left ear, but she recovered quickly and backed away from the attack. Strips of facial tissue flung around the place without a single scream. Red hair wrapped around the flayed skull and increased the fast chomping. A couple more shots were fired from the dying officer, some hitting the glass, and then the floor. The top of his uniform was stained with his raw flesh. It didn't take long for his legs to give way. Every limb quivered in agony. After two gushing bites, Blake dropped to the ground. All Monica could do was crawl aside, and aid her imprisoned team.

"BLAKE!" The remaining officer howled. Out of shock, Riggs stepped back to the room's wall, but was embraced by 106. Dark viscid matter swiftly consumed Riggs's trunk and limbs, promptly decomposing his features and turning him into a living skeleton.

Guiding Riggs's degraded hands, the old man took aim with the officers rifle and fired upon the frantic staff. Bullets sprayed into the helpless victims, killing most of the hysterical women. Those who survived joined Riggs as the ground overflowed with black mucus. It swallowed the injured party and left the echoes of their suffering along with residual damage around the chamber.

"No…" Monica whispered in defeat.

The clicking of teeth reminded her of the present danger. Monica noticed the vile creation, levitating towards her. Oiled intensities swayed as the decapitated fiend approached. Its mouth opened beyond human capacity, ready to eat once more.

Monica slowly slumped into the corner and accepted her doom, "This is how it ends."

Bloody choppers flew at the helpless maiden accompanied with a deafening shriek, but Monica did not flinch or show fear. That was until whips of lead barreled through Jessica's profile. Her evil spirit bursting to pieces in front of the stunned Director. Hot ink showered onto Monica's tidy outfit, which boiled away a large section of polyester and cotton, revealing her curved features. Blemished legs propped the ravishing dame up and towards two gentle hands. Officer Trung caught the swaying lass, and held her tight, while uttering one word: "Krasue."

"Thank you." The half-naked Director sniveled.

Trung regained some awareness and observed the gory scene: "What-what happened to everyone else?"

"106 took them."

By the end of the sentence, Monica had begun to weep.

"Oh god," Trung gasped at the revelation. He then turned and spotted the mauled supervisor, "Blake…"

Monica wiped away her tearful appearance. She then acknowledged in a formal posture, "106 must've conjured it, he's done that before,"

The sole surviving officer stood over his kill, which was melting away in the molten tar. On that occasion, he proved to be a real gunslinger of the Midwest. Under his shoulder Trung tucked a steaming M4A1, which he hastily reloaded and then reset. His hand lifted to adjust the tinted visor, and presented his striking jawline.

"My mother-she told me about the Krasue since I was young. She told me to be careful coming home late at night, or it would find me and use its long tongue to rip out my eyes. She said it was a cursed ancient princess. A headless vampire… So, if that was created by death magic, what else can be real?"

The very thought frightened him but evoked Monica to speak the absolute truth: "As long as 106 is free, I don't know. He's an interdimensional-necromancer, and must be stopped."

"The broadcast was successfully transmitted to all stations. MTF squadrons are on their way. ETA 20 minutes."

The director squinted at her inferior, "They won't be here in time."

"So what should we do?" Trung nervously inquired.

Monica exited the conversation, her focus drifted beyond the checkpoint.

"In this facility, there's another chance. Right next to Chamber 4-1, there's another variant for 106. A secondary containment area, composed of spherical cells that are randomly assembled by supports and different surfaces."

Director Grey paused and walked to Blake's remains. She snagged her ID from the deadman's grip, and then continued: "Both containment areas were under 24 hour surveillance by me. Any entity derived from 106 is unable to teleport from chamber 4-2, although at the time we believed the lead lined steel in 4-1 would do the trick."

"Can we trap it?!"

Trung grew paranoid and quickly checked his blind spots. He had an uneasy feeling that they were being watched. A part of him wanted to flee, but his duty prevailed. Protecting the director had become the man-at-arms priority, on top of stopping 106. Monica witnessed a courageous aura surround the tactical officer. Going forward, the director had a contagious smirk.

"Indeed. Follow me. I have a plan."

CHAPTER 6

"Have you ever been caught between the devil and the deep blue sea?"

That line finally resonated within Director Grey after all these years. Though Poe had lacked historical accuracy, the story was effective at inspiring fear through its use of senses. At the time of her first reading of *The Pit and the Pendulum*, Monica was mixed and rather confused on why the famed poet spared the nameless character.

"Why let him escape?" She pondered.

Death is more real than one could imagine. It was inevitable. She knew the real ending. The pendulum would've sliced the narrator open. A slow and painful death that was bestowed upon the condemned. Anyone in that position had to be there for a reason. She had always imagined the tortured were deserving of their affliction. Even so, in her aged heart, she knew David had changed that belief. Monica didn't want to accept the guilt, but it was there. She even gave Blake credit for making her feel responsible. Maybe if Director Grey owned up, she could finally be free.

However, she had her own priorities. Monica's escaped subject had killed her entire staff and security team, with exception of Trung and herself. It's current whereabouts were unknown and her only option was to secure the entity in its alternate containment chamber.

Being the director of Site 11, this was Monica's true responsibility. Endowed members are in charge of locating and containing individuals, entities, locations, and objects that violate natural law. The foundation's higher ups relied on Director Grey to make sure that objects 106 and 986 were secured for their research. Notorious anomalies located in Colorado: the old residents and the unpublished manuscript entitled Absent Willows.

Monica's discoveries were monumental. Her methods were adaptive and because of her local history, she was obsessed with one far more than the other. That is what gave her purpose. She worked too hard to lose everything.

In order to reach chamber 4-2, the survivors retraced their steps through the main corridor. Officer Trung remained beside Director Grey and kept a tight distance. Although the hallways were spacious, the establishment was located in a hollowed mountain and brought about claustrophobic sensations. With the addition of the looming evil that stalked them, both individuals were on high alert and in a hurry.

"I don't understand, Director. I thought 106 only went after depressed boys..." Trung couldn't fathom the recent murders.

Monica gave the officer a sideways glance, "Most of them. The G.I. is different."

"The G.I.?" Trung's eyes widened.

"Yes, a Corporal who lived in this very town."

They crossed the grated hall finding three marked-doors, which respectively led to the Surveillance room, Containment Zone, and Intro Office. Large rectangular gates contrasted with the tight-metal corridors shaped like cylinders. Monica hastily swiped her key card to unlock the central inlet.

Following her into the Containment Zone, Trung lowered his head and deduced, "...the others were also residents. Okay, so why only them? Why is he different?"

The director's eyes gleamed at the tactical officer. Her supple lips flouted, "Don't mistake me. The corporal still prefers depressed males between the ages of 10 to 25, but he controlled the others, making sure they only had that particular taste."

A perplexed Trung squeezed the forward grip of his carbine and set it to a semi-automatic firing mode. Then he feebly asked, "Why?"

"More for him if you think about it," Monica clarified with a subtle shrug.

Cold shivers rolled down Trungs spine. The very image of the slaughtered unit caused him to quiver. He respected Blake and felt his demise was grossly unfair. After the creature attacked, Commanding Officer Blake was left with an open crater for a face.

"I don't want to think about it."

"Well you should, he's hunting us now. We need to keep moving," Monica argued. She turned her head toward the passageway and extended her stride. A loud thump from overhead startled the two. Without delay Trung halted, squatted, and focused his crosshairs above to a flickering bulb.

"Come on," She urged.

Lightning in the distance startled the marksman. Incandescent lamps bursted one by one, followed by a swarm of darkness. Trung leapt up, but couldn't find his footing. He was engrossed by a pale face peeking through the blackness. A monochrome boy grinned like a Cheshire Cat and slowly approached. It's whimsical gestures were strange and unusual as if the child didn't possess a skeletal body. Struck with panic, Trung remained motionless, awaiting the unknown. Dainty hands gasped the officers patch and swiftly pulled him inside before locking the door.

"Do you need to be reminded? He's not agile. We need to keep moving!"

"Was that…?" He gasped.

Alluring-blue eyes twinkled with a pretty impatience. Trung stayed inert and transfixed on the director's beauty until it was uncomfortable. Lowering his head, the man-at-arms exhaled, "Sorry."

Director Grey angrily turned ahead to a flight of stairs which then led to a room split into three compartments. One served as a control area and the other two acted as containment chambers for 106. Characterized by its rudimentary style catwalk and concrete roof, the entire room consisted of computer servers and a small control area with beeping-control panels. Officer Trung lethargically trailed and examined the two large windows looking into both chambers.

"You've been studying 106 for a long time huh?" He uttered while staring into his dark reflection. His eyes were black as night.

"He predates 986" Monica returned as she flipped a level to lift the lockdown off the zone, granting access to containment chamber 4-2.

"Ah, I see. That's a long time."

Director Grey laughed at the officer's curiosity and carried on with her mission unbothered. Officer Trung went along and clinched his teeth.

"How old are you, Director?" He naively requested.

She professed, "Oh Trung, you should know- never ask a woman about her age."

"Haha, yeah I guess I should've known."

Before he could finish, Monica snapped her fingers and crudely ordered him to focus. Trung shook his head in embarrassment and breathed out steadily.

"I've just heard rumors you know."

Tow-colored hair waived in the gust of the egress. This was it. Now all she needed to do was create a diversion. Something that could lure this beast inside the cage and trap it indefinitely. Monica's head stirred, but her heart exclaimed, "We're here!"

Unperturbed, she held out her palm and beseeched, "Hand me your side arm."

This blindsided the young ally and caused him to turn his head in bewilderment.

"What?"

"I need to lure 106 in. If I'm successful, I'll need that to save me from a painful death."

Although he was filled with uncertainty, the guard reluctantly agreed. Trung released the forward grip of his rifle and lowered his arm to the left side holster.

"Here you go."

Director Grey took the handgun with extreme force. After a quick smile, Monica briefly strolled into the empty pit and hollered, "CORPORAL LAWRENCE GREY!! WHY DID YOU KILL THEM?!?"

Ear-splitting cackles alerted Tactical Officer Trung. The old man appeared behind him. An elderly humanoid with advanced rotting qualities was visible in all his forms. When Trung turned to open fire, Monica instantly shot the loyal guard in the back of the head. The bullet popped through his right eye and incapacitated the hapless chap. She punctually dragged his limp body into the room and then gestured the creature over. Trung immediately regained awareness and tried to defend himself against 106 with a pocket pistol from his boot. Unfortunately, the bullets didn't affect the old man, who promptly ripped out the officer's femur with a half-suppressed laugh. Officer Trung was slowly dismembered by the corporal as his screams were followed by weeping.

"I had to Red, it was my only choice," Monica whispered as she closed the doors. Blackness swallowed the room, and all that remained were the sounds of gnawing with childlike giggles.

Several months later, in another town, Elijah McBride was trying to quiet his infant daughter while talking with a divorce attorney. Unbeknownst, an old man was latched onto the wall, watching them and smiling.

Dante J. Martinez is a Colorado Native and writer. In his own words:

"I always had a knack for drawing really messed up images, but I wanted to develop from that, and express real feelings through writing and storytelling. Horror, Thrillers and Mysteries feel natural to me. Coincidence?"

Christina J. Moore is a Colorado illustrator and designer. In her own words:

"As a passionate artist, I strive for skill, and as an avid storyteller, I seek to spread truth. As a growing illustrator, I aim to merge these two motivations in order to tell my own stories and those of others."

IMPERIO

Dante J. Martinez

www.ingramcontent.com/pod-product-compliance
Lightning Source LLC
Chambersburg PA
CBHW072128150726
47999CB00005B/2195